MAY 28 1985 Joe D.M.

SEP 6 1987 Rose Pfader

MAR 3 1992 Stephen Shih was here!

JUL 18 1997 Matthew Allen

JAN 28 1996 PandaErica

APR 3 1999 Arthur Curry

$1.00 FINE FOR BOOKS

RETURNED WITHOUT

DATE CARDS.

All original artwork by the world's most famous artist,

ARTHUR CURRY

THE
MYSTERY
OF
ATLANTIS

ARTHUR'S ~~MYSTERY~~ GUIDE TO ATLANTIS

ARTHUR CURRY
by ~~Bernard Collins~~

HARPER

An Imprint of HarperCollinsPublishers

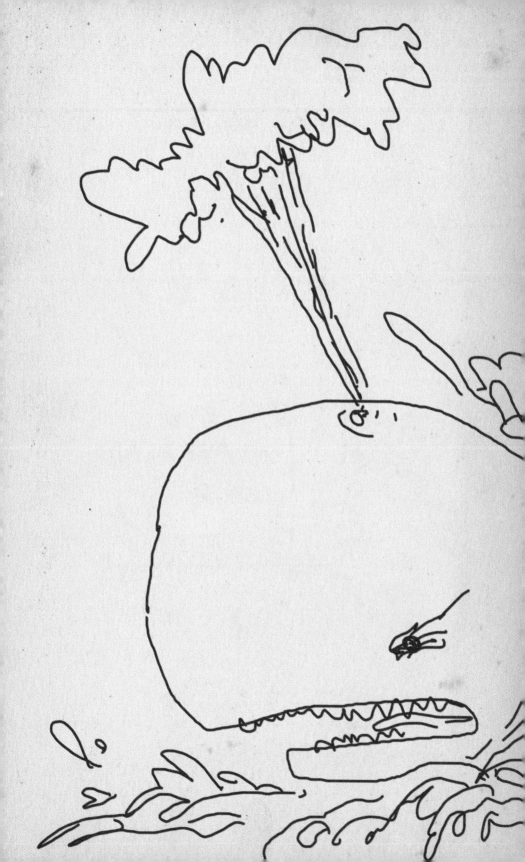

IF YOU ARE READING THIS, TURN BACK NOW.
THAT MEANS YOU... DAD!

ALL RIGHT, let's face it. I don't have a ton of friends, but just in case someone besides my dad finds this book, I need you to know that what you're about to read may possibly change your life *forever.*

It definitely changed mine.

I used to believe the guy who wrote this book. Bernard Collins. It seemed like he knew a lot about Atlantis, but then I started experiencing **WEIRD STUFF.** . .

I know it sounds crazy **(AND IT IS)** but my mom is from Atlantis. But not the boring version Bernie writes about. The **REAL** Atlantis.

Along with the stories my dad told me and some new stories from an unexpected friend, I pulled everything I could find on my ocean adventures and put it all in this book. So **seriously.** If you're reading this and you're not an Atlantean like me, **STOP!**

Aquaman created by
Paul Norris and Mort Weisinger

Text and editorial by Alexandra West
Book design by Erica De Chavez

Aquaman: Arthur's Guide to Atlantis
Copyright © 2018 DC Comics
AQUAMAN and all related characters and elements © & ™
DC Comics and Warner Bros. Entertainment Inc.
(s18)

HARP41452

Photo Credits:
The folloing photograph © Getty Images: page 117, Deep sea
exploratory 1892. The following photographs, paintings, and
engravings © Shutterstock: page 13, birthday card; page 15, map of
ancient Greece; page 17, marble statue of Poseidon; page 80, old
coins; page 87, pressed flowers; pages 90-91, ancient Greek scene;
page 123, 1970's scuba divers; page 134, key; page 135, old man.

TABLE of CONTENTS

Part I

The Rise of Atlantis

The typical student of history or science will most likely never encounter a myth, tale, epic, and legend so persistent or so imaginatively powerful as that of the great island-continent of Atlantis. Sunken miles deep beneath the waves of the cold, unforgiving sea, this lost civilization has been studied in earnest for good reason.

Even with each passing millennia, instead of being lost to the dusty library shelves, Atlantis has become a scientific probability. This new information compels the attention of the serious scientist and historian, of which I am both.

Over the course of this book, I will be making powerful arguments for and against the existence of Atlantis. Only when we shine a light upon both sides of an argument do we begin to see the truth.

HAPPY FLIPPIN' BIRTHDAY TO ME!!!

I'm 13 today, which means I'm a teenager now. My dad surprised me this morning with life preserver-shaped pancakes. Yes, I told him that pancakes are already shaped like life preservers, but he said these have holes in the middle like a REAL life preserver. SO I basically ate flat donuts. BUT I did get an awesome present!

I got my very own **CAMERA!**

SHE'S BEAUTIFUL!

Canon 7S Rangefinder with a 50mm lens. If I could write the sound of me whistling, I would.

And this book is the perfect place to fill up with the photos I'm going to take. My dad gave this to me a while ago. He said this book would teach me a lot about Atlantis, and he would tell me more about my mom.

PLUS my language arts teacher told us that we should be writing every day. Not only am I "exercising my composition skills" (rolling my eyes) but I can also keep all my Atlantis knowledge in one place!

TOM PAL
Greeting Cards
www.tompalcards.com

Made with love in the U.S.A.
Portland, OR 97239

8 53923 00473

and in earnest
en with each
hly the same
se of the lost
red to be about
world around
our modern
around them,
mathematics,
loser to them
closer to the
do we begin
short period,
heant that of
rope or even
otice classical
mation today
d in earnest
with each
the ancient
this short
interpreting,
g this point.

HAPPY BIRTHDAY TO ME!

13

HAPPY BIRTHDAY

Beginning in 800 B.C., the era of Classic Antiquity is generally considered to be the origin point for many subsequent cultures, mainly influencing Western culture.

If you look around any city in Europe or even America, you'll not only notice classical Greek inspired architecture, but also many Greek inventions. The ancient Greeks invented necessities in our modern culture like infrastructure and democracy. Most importantly, the ancient Greeks spent most of their time collecting, interpreting, and recording knowledge. THE MOST BORING SUBJECT OF ALL TIME

The ancient Greeks saw mathematics as an essential part of life because they valued numerical precision. This concept was unheard of up until this point. Even with its relatively small population (estimated to be about ten million— roughly the same population as today!) and during this short period of time, Greece was able to advance in many fields of science, philosophy, mathematics, and history.

Why? Because to them, science and religion worked hand in hand. Understanding the world

Fig. I

MAP OF ANCIENT GREECE

I told my dad I didn't really want a birthday party. They seem pretty **LAME** when you get to my age, I mean, what are we gonna do, play pin the tail on the donkey? I'd rather be outside, cliff jumping or just hanging out on the dock.

Plus, I don't particularly like anyone in my class, or school, or . . . actually, I don't think I like people in general. Huh, I guess growing up means learning more about yourself.

COOL!

...t Greece was polytheistic, meaning that they believed in multiple gods and goddesses. There are twelve main deities. At the top of the heap, Zeus was called the king of the gods, due to his ability to control and influence the other immortals. Zeus was also god of the sky, and with that comes thunder and lightning. Hades was god of the underworld and wielded power over mortals' fates.

Then, of course, there was Poseidon, ruler of the sea, earthquakes, and horses. In a country with 13,676 km (8,497 miles) of coastline, including thousands of inhabited islands, Poseidon was an ever-present figure in daily Greek life.

Fig. II
MARBLE STATUE OF POSEIDON
WITH TRIDENT

My dad has always been the quiet type, so I *know* not to ask him a *ton* of questions about my mom.

But this one time, when we were sitting out on the dock watching the sunset, he told me the story of how they met. He talked about how a MASSIVE storm rolled in and raged through the long night. He hadn't seen anything like it before. He said the walls of the lighthouse *shook* and the waves threatened to crash up and over the cliff side.

Then suddenly, he spotted something STRANGE in the water. He said that he could barely make out a mysterious figure lying against a flat rock. It looked like an unconscious woman. When he made his way down to the beach and lifted her from the water, he noticed that she was clutching a long metal object.

re
th
is
rc
i
s

With the light from the bolts of lightning, he said he was able to make out her features. She was injured, but he noted that the wounds looked to be from something more powerful than just the shoreline rocks. My dad carried her across the beach and up toward the house. When they finally made it inside, my dad got a better look at the object in her hand.

It was a beautiful silver trident!

A REAL ONE.

> Thinking about it now,
> I wish he had taken a
> picture of it. Just so
> I could have one more
> memory of my mom.

...like Corinth where Poseidon was the chief god, people prayed to the god for their ship's safe voyage. Sometimes they would even drown horses as a sacrifice.

WAIT, WHAT?!?! HARSH!

Practically every major city in Greece had a chief god. Not surprisingly, they most often correlated with the major export or geograph... instance, the capital city of At... with Athena, goddess of wisdo... of war with Delphi.

War isn't EXACTLY an export. Delphi and their guy Apollo sound like guys just playing battleship. Or Dungeons and Dragons.

Although Poseidon and his f... immortal, they couldn't exactly do... they wanted with a snap of their... were tied to their fates, meaning that everything's life was mapped from...

end by the fates. The gods were unable to change or control their destinies. For example, in Homer's *The Odyssey*, it was the main character's fate to return home safely. The gods could only place obstacles in his path. They could not stop him.

Ultimately, ancient Greek science and religion made its culture extremely conducive to studying and debating new ways of thinking. And as the civilization grew, so did a burgeoning community of philosophers.

Classical students prepared in earnest for
reason. Even with each passin

the sam

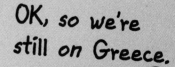

OK, so we're still on Greece. **LAME.** What does this have to do with Atlantis?

One of those philosophers was named Plato. Founder of the Academy in Athens, widely regarded as the first institution of higher education at the time, Plato played a pivotal role in our modern Western culture. Mainly by developing an entirely new way of looking at philosophy, ~~still relevant~~ today some 2,4000

THIS IS GETTING BORING.

I've got WAY more interesting stuff going on. Since Dad has been letting me do stuff on my own now, like walk home from school, go the arcade, and go swimming, I've been getting some really GREAT pictures with my new camera. I took one of the lighthouse on my way home. It looks like something you'd see in a magazine or something!

I guess it's pretty cool to live in an ACTUAL lighthouse. When I was younger, I thought everyone lived in a lighthouse on their own cliffs. Now that I think about it, that's WAY too many lighthouses. The entire coastline would be like Times Square!

I don't even know how long our lighthouse has been here. Probably since Plato. Ships have been coming through here for ages, and without our lighthouse they would crash into the rocks. Then we would have some ghost ships on our hands . . . then WHO YA GONNA CALL? GHOSTBUSTERS! Such a good movie! I watched it for basically the hundredth time last night.

I would be the greatest Ghostbuster to ever live because not only am I not afraid of NO GHOSTS, I'm not afraid of anything.

Call me, fellas.

EXAMPLE #1 of how I'm not afraid of anything. I stole a harpoon from the **BIGGEST, CRUSTIEST** fisherman down by the docks. It was just *hanging* off his fishing boat, asking to be taken. It was crazy. He didn't even turn around—he was busy looking at something in the water. Then **BOOM**, I snatched it and took off. Now I just need two more and maybe I can make them into a trident!

i_____ writes at this time and gives the world the first mention of the lost city of Atlantis. **YES! ATLANTIS!**

FINALLY!!!
HERE WE GO!

ἓν ὑπερέχει μεγέθει καὶ ἀρετῇ:
λέγει γὰρ τὰ γεγραμμένα ὅσην
ἡ πόλις ὑμῶν ἔπαυσέν ποτε
δύναμιν ὕβρει πορευομένην
ἅμα ἐπὶ πᾶσαν Εὐρώπην καὶ
Ἀσίαν, ἔξωθεν ὁρμηθεῖσαν
ἐκ τοῦ Ἀτλαντικοῦ πελάγους.
τότε γὰρ πορεύσιμον ἦν τὸ
ἐκεῖ πέλαγος: νῆσον γὰρ πρὸ
τοῦ στόματος εἶχεν ὃ καλεῖτε,
ὥς φατε, ὑμεῖς Ἡρακλέους
στήλας, ἡ δὲ νῆσος ἅμα Λιβύης
ἦν καὶ Ἀσίας μείζων, ἐξ ἧς
ἐπιβατὸν ἐπὶ τὰς ἄλλας νήσους
τοῖς τότε ἐγίγνετο πορευομ

It's all Greek to me...

EARLY TWENTIETH CENTURY ENGLISH TRANSLATION

For it is related in our records how once upon a time your State stayed the course of a mighty host, which, starting from a distant point in the Atlantic ocean, was insolently advancing to attack the whole of Europe, and Asia to boot. For the ocean there was at that time navigable; for in front of the mouth which you Greeks call, as you say, "the pillars of Heracles," there lay an island which was larger than Libya and Asia together; and it was possible for the travelers of that time to cross from it to the other islands, and from the islands to the whole of the continent over against them which encompasses that veritable ocean.

I'm lost

For all that we have here, lying within the mouth of which we speak, is evidently a haven having a narrow entrance; but that yonder is a real ocean, and the land surrounding it may most rightly be called, in the fullest and truest sense, a continent.

Now in this island of Atlantis there existed a confederation of kings, of great and marvelous power, which held sway over all the island, and over many other islands.

Hmmmm, many other islands? Could there be multiple kingdoms in Atlantis?

BOOM!!

The most intriguing part of this dialogue from Plato is that he claims in his introduction that he is quoting an Athenian statesman who went to Egypt, and while he was there, translated actual Egyptian records of the existence of Atlantis. Basically that means Plato seems to be genuinely referencing an actual republic.

Plato uses Atlantis as an example of how imperfect its attributes were when compared to his perfect theoretical republic. Note the "confederation of kings, of great and marvelous power, which held sway over all the island, and over many other islands also and parts of the continent" doesn't sound like the best form of government when we are at a time in human history where democracy is seen as a revolutionary idea. A confederation of kings would feel like a step backwards for ancient Greeks, making Atlantis a powerful argumentative tool for Plato but also leaving its reader with lingering questi-

AND QUEENS LIKE MY MOM

Yeah, like ME. Here's one question, why would a group of kings and queens getting together and hashing things out be so BAD? Seems pretty efficient to me.

EXAMPLE #2 of how I'm not afraid of anything. We had a HUGE storm last night and even though my dad told me not to, I snuck out to get it on film. The lightning cracked across the sky at the PERFECT moment—it was so sick. But the storm reminded me, I forgot to finish the story about my mom.

y_____ This new
i

After my dad brought her inside, he dried her off and treated her wounds. He let her sleep for a while so she could recover, until she woke up frightened and confused. My dad said she was super strong, so strong she THREW HIM AGAINST A WALL and blew up his TV! Eventually she realized my dad was only there to help, and she began to trust him. She told him that her name was ATLANNA, QUEEN OF ATLANTIS.

pro

Yeah, you read that right, **QUEEN**! So I guess that makes me a prince, right? Doesn't sound right. The only princes I know are those cheesy prince charmings. And I am definitely NOT a prince charming.

The details are kind of fuzzy, but Dad said she was *running away* from Atlantis, that they were *forcing* her to marry some king she didn't want to marry. She asked if she could stay at the lighthouse for a while, and my dad said yes (which I was surprised to hear—he's usually such a grouch). Then, ya know, they fell in love and stuff. **BLEGH.**

Then poof! They had me.

But when I was three, Mom and Dad were **ATTACKED.** Atlantean guards had found her and tried to take her back. My dad says mom made a very difficult decision. She had to go back. She had to leave us to *protect* us.

I've never told anyone this story before, and now that I'm writing it out, it's making me feel . . . sad.

Sunken miles deep beneath the seri...
Greek inspired archit...
spent most likely nev...
...bic, and historian, of...
...sty library shelves, A...
...odern culture and ag...
...as become a scientific p...

So after last night's storm, I found this bottle that washed up on shore! Looks like there's a super-old map inside. Honestly, it doesn't look human. It looks ANCIENT but alien at the same time. Wow, maybe this book is getting to my head. It couldn't be **Atlantean** . . . could it? Too much of a coincidence.

THE TIMELINE

How an Idea Spread

DINOSAURS, I GUESS???

Volcanic eruption caused a large tsunami that wiped out the island of Crete

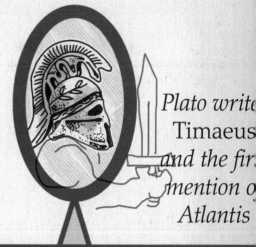

Plato write
Timaeus
and the fir.
mention o
Atlantis

| 1600 B.C. | 800 B.C. | 360 B.C. |

Greek Dark Age ends and Classic Antiquity Begins

MUMMIES

OF ATLANTIS:
Through the Ages

Renaissance Utopian Francis Bacon writes New Atlantis

200 A.D. | 1627 A.D. | 1898 A.D.

...oticus writes ...n epic poem based on Atlantis

American poet Edith Willis Linn Forbes writes "The Lost Atlantis"

1986 A.D.—APPARENTLY A PRINCE WAS BORN (me?!?)

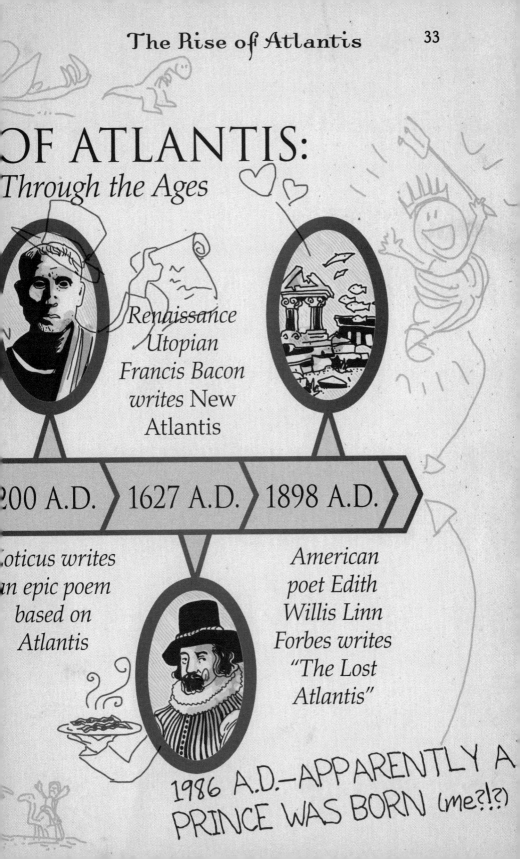

PART II

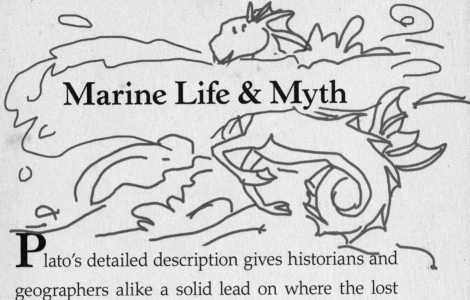

Marine Life & Myth

Plato's detailed description gives historians and geographers alike a solid lead on where the lost city may be located. If you explore and essentially break down Plato's text and compare it to maps, writings, and oral histories of the time, a new image of Atlantis emerges.

When Atlantis is placed in the context of the animal life and ecosystem surrounding the land, that helps us get an approximate location of the grouping of islands.

For years, people have imagined the scenes, above and below the water, using both the primary sources of Plato and additional modern research. Exploring these facets of the mystery, one can only learn more by taking a deeper dive into the landscape of Atlantis.

Mission Statement

Our mission at Boston Museum is to be a world leader in engaging and educating the community about the history of marine life, oceans and waterways. We aim to educate and inspire future generations to support the conservation of all marine life, oceans and waterways.

As fierce advocates of ocean and marine conservation, we have an opportunity to inspire change and create breakthroughs using scientific research undertaken in our centre of excellence to ensure future generations have the opportunity to carry on our research and continue to protect all marine life and prevent future destruction.

We all play a role and share the responsibility to take care of the ocean. oday, the future of the ocean is in our hands. Forward generations depend on our overall actions now to ensure that we have a healthy and abundant ecosystem to sustain life well into the future

Boston Aquarium
OF THE SEA

Information desk is l
Toliets including diable
floor. Do not open fire
an emergency.

THE ATRIU

1 The Deep

2 Tropical

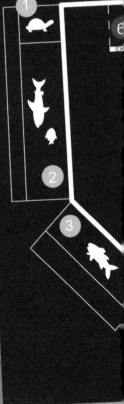

t the vistor
desk for a
f information
guided tours.

ground floor.
ated on every
in the case of

5 Amenities

6 Exit

Welcome to:

Boston
Aquarium
OF THE SEA

My class is going to the aquarium today, and I'm
SO EXCITED, even though we basically take
this field trip every year. Obviously, I'm a big fan of
the ocean, and water, and fish—just about everything
marine. My teacher told us to bring a sketch pad so
that we can take rubbings of all of the information.
I probably won't need it, though. I pretty much know
everything there is to know about sea life. I'm
sneaking in my camera and this book so I can figure
out which fish might be swimming around
in Atlantis. . . .

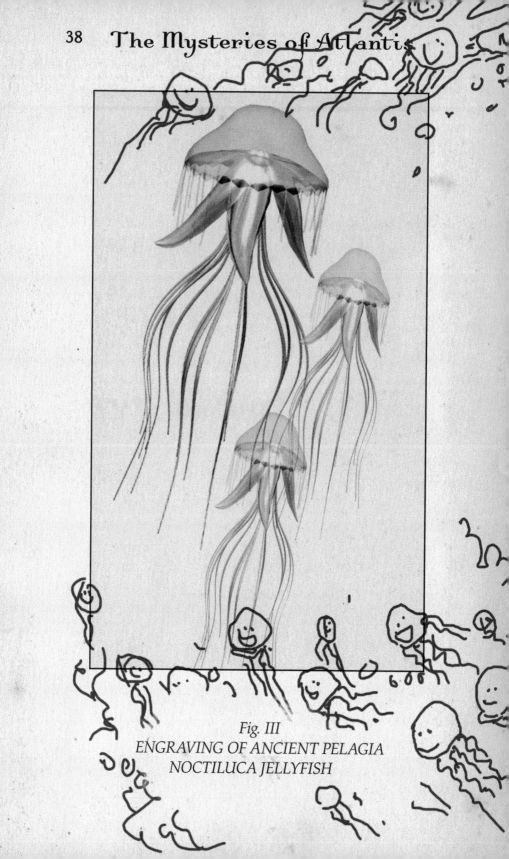

Fig. III
ENGRAVING OF ANCIENT PELAGIA
NOCTILUCA JELLYFISH

JELLYFISH SPOTTING!

The *Pelagia noctiluca* jellyfish would have been (and still is) the most common species of jellyfish in the Mediterranean Sea, the most widely accepted location of Atlantis. Known throughout Europe as the mauve stinger, not only can this sea creature sting, this particular species is also celebrated for its ability to glow in the dark.

By studying the ocean's inhabitants, we can begin to see how Atlanteans would have lived during Plato's time and well before. Given that it was a small continent with an enormous coastline, we can assume Atlantis's main food source would have been the fish that inhabited their waters. Despite what we may think, the act of whaling wouldn't come into vogue until the eighteenth century

Today the tour guide asked us: If you could be *any* sea creature, what would you be?

A. Orca (Also known as the killer whale! I want to see a real one someday!)

B. Great white shark (ever seen *JAWS*?)

C. Manta ray (very flat, but can sting)

D. All of the above.

The correct answer (and the one I chose) is *obviously* D: ALL OF THE ABOVE. But then I asked, would you be a great blue whale shark ray? Or would you be you but could change your form *any* time you wanted?

... but still an impressive 20 ft ...

... can begin to see how Atlantis' ...

Lamnidae

GREAT

Great White Sharks are the large...
water. They have a heavy torpedo...
of 3900ft. Great white sharks play...

ANATOMY

The great white shark has a robus...
replace any broken front teeth. Th...
sharks, the great white is able to d...
upper and lower parts of the tail a...
underside and gray dorsal area. T...
white pups are around 4ft. when...

BEHAVIOR

In some oceans, great white sharks...
and sharks are territorial to new sh...
means they lift their head above the...
whites swim at a high speed to get...
...sharks have the highest number of in...
...senses are in...

CONSERVAT...

...mbers have bec...
...etimes caught b...
...heir jaws and fi...
...ted as they have...

I used my pencil to do some rubbings of the plaques around the aquarium. These were my favorite exhibits!

WHITE SHARKS

...tory fish and can be found all major oceans, usually swimming in ...body and powerful tail which helps them swim up to 35 mph. Th... ...d role at the top of the ocean's food chain.

...conical snout and over 300 serrated teeth. Their teeth are in m... ...e their head side to side when eating to saw chunks of flesh fro... ...otromagnetic fields emitted by the movement of other animals. T... ...d the same size. Great white sharks are counter-shaded mean... ...e them when hunting. Female great white sharks grow bigger... ...grow 9in every year. They can grow up to 19ft. long.

...a dominance hierarchy; the females dominate males, larger... ...nlike other shark species the great white shark displays spy... ...to get a better view of the activity on the water's surface, in... ...momentum to propel themselves out of the water to catch s... ...s with humans, they do not seek out humans as prey. Many gre... ...In waters with low visibility. Studies show that sharks prefer...

...easing and they are now considered vulnerable. Humans re... ...ent in fishing nets and protective beach netting. They are also... ...cation is crucial in helping humans understand great whites ... ...e important role in the marine ecosystem.

Medusozoa JE

...y are an animal having roamed the seas for at...
...nidarian. There are more than 350 species of je...
...shaped body with tentacles whose length and...
...n eye the Irukandji to very large Lions Mane je...

...hey do not have a brain, bones, head or heart....
...ody is oxygenated by diffusion. They have lim...
...gh contraction-pulsations of the bell like body...
...Most of the umbrella mass is a gelatinous ma...
...skin. The top layer is called the epidermis, a...

POPULATION

...e carnivorous feeding on plankton, crustacea...
...t passively using their tentacles as driftnets. T...
...pture prey, when their body expands it displac...
...n the reach of their tentacles. Jellyfish popula...
...of their natural predators and the availability...

TY & TREATMENT OF STINGS

...the most famous for their ability to sting. Th...
...uces enough poison to kill 60 humans and is...
...or stings is Vinegar.

LYFISH

00 million years or more. They are
ound in every ocean from the very
depend on the species. They can
hat can be almost 8 feet wide and

sh do not need a respiratory system
ontrol over movement and use their
species actively swim most of the
the jelly called mesoglea which is
inner layer is referred to as gastro

eggs, small fish and other jellyfish.
yfish swimming technique also helps
re water which brings more potential
ay be expanding globally because of
cessive nutrients due to land run off.

venomous jellyfish is the box jellyfish
eason for 1 death per year. A common

So I kind of forgot to mention I have some bad memories at this aquarium. . . .

When I was nine, I was being pushed around by some kids. They said I was talking to the fish—which I wasn't! Or at least I think I wasn't. Sometimes when I get close to fish, I feel like I can feel them or sense how they feel. It sounds like this VUUUU VUUU VUUU noise.

(I'm doing a bad job of explaining this.

It's not weird or anything!)

But this time, when one of the giant tiger sharks saw the kids teasing me, I could feel him get really angry. Then all of a sudden the shark started to ram his head against the glass tank. HARD. Over and over again, he kept running into the glass until it began to crack! Everyone started to scream—the tank was going to break, and thousands of gallons of water were going to FLOOD the room.

But I wasn't scared. This *calm* feeling washed over me. It was like I knew everything was going to be all right. I put my hand on the glass and closed my eyes to try to calm or maybe focus on (?) the shark. And when I opened my eyes, suddenly all of the other sea creatures gathered around me. Then I turned around, I saw everyone's faces. They were all really freaked out.

I MEAN . . . I WAS, TOO!

Then when my teacher got everyone back on the bus, no one sat next me or looked at me.

It's like they were scared of me.

for their unique shells. The nautilus shell is one of the greatest

Fig. IV
ENGRAVING OF ANCIENT
HORNED NAUTILUS

The nautilus has been around for almost 500 million years, making it one of the oldest sea creatures known to man. With no real use for food or medicine, th~ people of Atlantis and the rest of the ancien~ ~~ ~d not have gone in search of the ~~~ ~nique shells. The naut~ natural exampl~ similar spiral mathematica~ be seen in example, t~ its prey, t~ to a lig~ of the shell~ or li~

My friend Claudia took this, it's a little dark but you can see behind me . . . it was so SCARY!

b~ and the~ mathematician Jaco~ *Mirabilis*, Bernoulli points out t~

no

When I got home from the aquarium, I was talking to Dad about all the **COOL** animals I'd seen, and he told me more stuff about Atlantis! I swear, this guy is keeping stuff from me on purpose.

He said that Mom used to talk about all the creatures that lived in Atlantis and how they **EVOLVED** from the creatures of our world.

Dad actually made me a list of all the different sea creatures in Atlantis from what he could remember from his conversations with Mom.

Mer-people
Jellyfish beings
Man-sized crustaceans
Giant seahorses
Cephalopod people

Sea, the most wide... regarded location...

I KNEW GIANT SEAHORSES WERE REAL!! I found this pic on the web when I was messing around in the school library. (They get dial up—we don't even have a computer at the lighthouse!) Some deep-sea diver took this picture and reported that he thought he saw a man riding it! Everyone thought he was crazy, but I think this is an *actual* Atlantean riding a SEAHORSE!

Sea myths have been around for centuries. They derive from old sailor tales of monsters erupting from the depths to destroy whole armadas. Whether we believe these tales to be true or not, if we are to explore the truth behind Atlantis, then these tales deserve our equal attention. The giant squid is the greatest example of myth becoming reality. Many thought this gigantic creature to be only the imaginings of mad sailors, until 1873, when an actual giant squid was caught off the coast of Newfoundland. Not fully grown but still an impressive 20 ft long, this was the first giant squid to ever be

It's been a while since I've written. I've been thinking a lot about the WEIRD things that have been happening to me. Who am I really? I'm supposed to be Atlantean, but it's hard when I'm not around other people like me.

It's like I have a *secret* identity.

But one, uh, person has been there for me. There's something I haven't told *anyone*, not even my dad. When I was little, I was sitting on the dock when out of nowhere a little tentacle plopped in front of me. And that was the beginning of a beautiful friendship with my pal Topo . . . **THE OCTOPUS!** Let's see if I find him. He's usually hanging around the dock. . . .

PART III

A Flawed Government

At the heart of Atlantis was a controversial governmental structure that has drawn great criticism—one of the ultimate critics being Plato himself. However, Plato shouldn't be worried, as this governmental ideology has never been put into practice.

If the stories are to be believed and Atlantis does in fact exist, then we can assume that this government is still in place. Perhaps deep under the ocean's waves, a monarchy still reigns supreme. With no direct evidence giving today's political and cultural scientists clues to Atlantis' government, whether successful or not, we can only exercise the theory in our minds.

If a failure, as Plato claimed, then Atlantis may have fallen before it ever began to take on water.

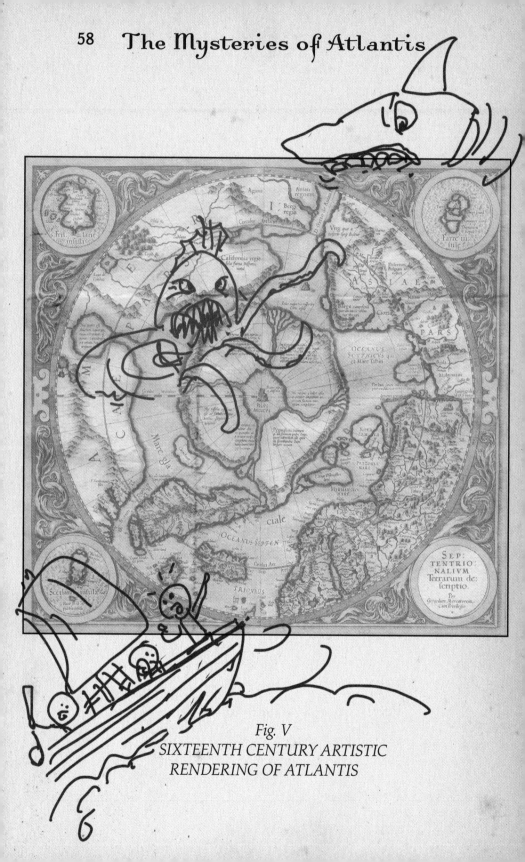

Fig. V
SIXTEENTH CENTURY ARTISTIC
RENDERING OF ATLANTIS

Atlantis was ruled by a confederation into the

GONE SWIMMING
(BECAUSE YOU DIDN'T FIX MY BIKE)

of those

centuries.

this govern

me tha

↑

The note I left on my dad's newspaper this morning that he didn't notice

WOW. So, UHHHHHH . . .
I JUST HAD A VERY
INTERESTING DAY. . . .

Where do I even start??

Basically, these *annoying* kids from school and their girlfriends dared me to swim down to this *sunken* ship. I'd seen the ship before, so I was pretty sure I could do it. I can hold my breath longer than *anyone* at school.

(Plus, I kinda have a **HUGE** crush on one of the girls who was there so . . . I might have also been trying to show off a little.)

So I swam down to the sunken ship (which was a lot farther down than I'd thought) and managed to get *inside* the hull. I wanted to bring something back up to the surface so no one could say I hadn't done it. I immediately spotted this old candlestick and went for it, but when I went to grab it, suddenly this **HUGE GIGANTIC MORAY EEL** started to attack me!

Next thing I knew, I was stuck inside the ship. I was starting to run out of breath, so I banged my fists against the broken door until everything went **BLACK.**

I THOUGHT I WAS DEAD. SUPER DEAD.

Then I remember opening my eyes. It was murky at first, but then my eyes started to focus, and I realized I was STILL underwater. How could that be real? My first thought was heaven is underwater, which would make sense. But if I was in heaven, why did my fists hurt so much?

Then I thought: This isn't heaven. I'm not dead. I'm breathing.

UNDERWATER.

Then I looked up toward the surface, and I saw . . . *a man!*

He knew my name. He told me he'd been looking for me for a long time.

When I asked who he was and if he knew my mom, he hesitated. Then said:

My name is Vulko, and I'm the chief scientific adviser to the great civilization of Atlantis. It is time you learned about your people, young prince.

So YEAH, a lot happened today. BUT let the record SHOW . . .

I still managed to get my candlestick.

My first thought after I met Vulko was . . . I can't believe I'm meeting an *actual* **ATLANTEAN!** And he's calling **ME** a prince! So all those stories my dad has been telling me are actually **REAL?!** I mean, I believed my dad, but now *everything* has changed. It's all real.

Although we can plant our feet on the fact that Atlantis was ruled by a confederation of kings, **AND QUEENS AND PRINCES** we don't know much about how they defended their continent or kept the peace. Assuming the culture to be similar to that of ancient Greece, they had a military and they outfitted that military with weapons. No artifacts exist today, but we can continue our investigation into the daily life of an Atlantean by theorizing **YES THEY DO**

LOOK! I managed to snag a picture of Vulko and his spear. He would kill me if he knew I took a picture of him . . . wait, do you think he knows what a picture is? Anyway, he says that I'll get to the use the spear **IN OUR TRAINING!**

Last week, Vulko brought something else to the surface. It felt like leather, but it was black and rubbery. I asked him what it was, and he said it was sharkskin. Let me repeat that. SHARKSKIN. It's how they write stuff down in Atlantis.

There has also been a question I've been wanting to ask Vulko, but the time hasn't been right. So I just blurted it out. Maybe I was scared of the answer. I asked him about my mom and if he knew where she was.

He just said he'll tell me more about my mom when I'm ready.

Whatever that means.

the strongest of the fundamental structure of this ancient continent. The "confederation of kings" is what modern political scientists would call a confederation power structure coupled with a monarchial sociopolitical ideology. The most intriguing aspect of this theoretical government would be the competing royal families.

It's been three weeks since I first met Vulko, and he *still won't* let me do anything **FUN.** What gives? Just like my dad, who Vulko asked about. Apparently, they already know each other!! My dad is going to have some explaining to do tonight.

But I guess Vulko **HAS** been teaching me about Atlantis. Did you know there were **SEVEN KINGDOMS?**

I KNEW IT.

I made my own charts so I can keep track.

Every other day, Vulko has been bringing different weapons to the surface to teach me about each kingdom. Check out these GREAT pictures I've gotten. When Vulko asked what my camera was, I just told him it was a human thing that he wouldn't understand. I've organized them in order of kingdom, and I've added as much information as I could remember from talking to Vulko.

ATLANTIS
Ruled by King Atlan
(Really the "spirit" of Atlan, since he's dead. Basically, he's a really strong ghost king.)

1ST

The two largest cities are Poseidonis and Tritonis

This is something
called a shock pole!

Atlan

antis d
re critic
d, the
wea
un

Hydro-pulse rifle

XEBEL
Ruled by King Nereus

Vulko says the king has a family. Apparently, he has a daughter my age named Mera. Kinda sorta jealous that she's down there and I'm up here.

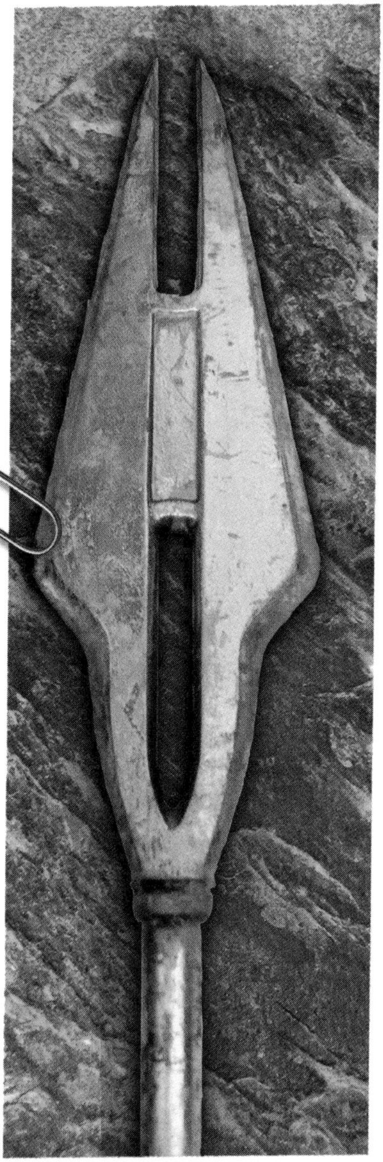

Xebellian polearm

ato shouldn't
Atlantis does
act exist, they
s. No artifacts

ruled by a controversial

has never began to take

can pl   t es ra

Very important Xebels travel by seahorse or sea dragon (you know, like you do).

FISHERMEN

FACT: They're known for their minds. They are a kingdom filled with artists and theorists. They believe in love not war. They would rather educate than destroy their enemies.

Similar to the Brine, the Fishermen exhibit signs of aquatic mutation.

THE BRINE

The Brine are a proud and strong kingdom. They will defend their home at all costs. They're united, strong, and will protect their own.

Extremely effected by aquatic evolution, the Brine have taken on the appearance and physical abilities of the typical crustacean.

Strong military might.

THE DESERTERS

They broke off from all the other kingdoms and were lost to time. Known for forging mighty weapons—their location is unknown.

The Deserters were the first to leave after Atlantis fell. Seeing no way for the kingdoms to unite after the tragedy of King Atlan, they left to create their own society.

THE TRENCH
Ruled by ??

Just a heads-up, there will be a lot of question marks for these last two.

There's not a lot known about the Trench, just that the things that live there live in total darkness. They've adapted by eating small creatures, and Vulko said some even glow in the dark!

KINGDOM #7
A.K.A. THE LOST KINGDOM
Ruled by ??

When I asked about the seventh and final kingdom, Vulko clammed up. He said no one knows what happened to them. That one day they just disappeared.

SPOOKY!!

Vulko made me this ancient engraving of what a Trench creature might look like!

Part IV

Life in Atlantis

What we know about the daily life of an Atlantean, probable or not, is a mystery not only due to the lack of records of its existence but because the daily life of any inhabitant of the ancient western world is difficult to confirm.

With no form of writing besides tablets or depiction besides expensive sculptures, the ancient world has been subject to immense scientific and historical speculation. From the food they ate, to the clothes they wore, to the way they got around, today's minds have painted a clearer picture for us through archaeological clues.

Whether or not it even existed, we can still get an idea of how Atlantis once was before its ultimate destruction.

Around this time, when it came to clothing, the style really depended on the job or function of the person who was wearing it. We can assume in Atlantis that ~~there were many different types of clothing worn because of the changing climates in the Mediterranean Sea. But each garment was just a different iteration of the basic tunic.~~

NOPE

I mean, how would people underwater swim around with tunics? You gotta wear something with a sleeker design. Vulko told me that everyone in Atlantis wears these high-tech suits that make you swim even FASTER.

I mean, just look at his suit: it looks like the scales of a fish. So I guess that's what inspired its design—makes sense!

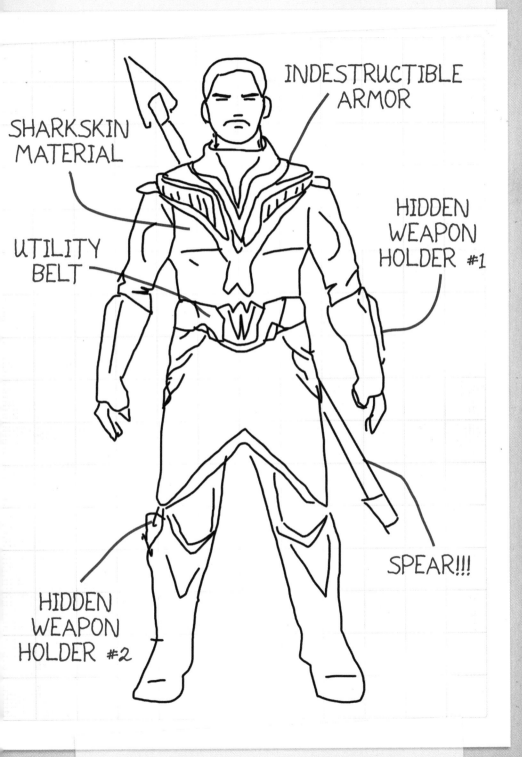

SHARKSKIN MATERIAL

INDESTRUCTIBLE ARMOR

HIDDEN WEAPON HOLDER #1

UTILITY BELT

HIDDEN WEAPON HOLDER #2

SPEAR!!!

Three hundred years before Plato's time, ancient Greece switched from a bartering system to a coin system. That means that each city (or city-state) began to produce their own coin. If Atlantis was anything like similar ancient cultures, it's around this time that they began to produce their own currency as well.

The coins pictured below are believed to be true Atlantean coin. The face of the coin would have depicted a leader, most likely whichever king was ruler of that city-state. The opposing face held an image that honored the fishing industry.

OR QUEEN OR PRINCE

$

$

Fig. VI
FOUND ANCIENT COIN
[BELIEVED TO BE ATLANTEAN]

Atlantis, 300 years before Plato's time, ancient

Vulko showed me some of the coins from a bag he brought to the surface.

These are real,
GENUINE
Atlantean coins!

are

sc

difficult to

th   comi

pensive

anyt

ent

you

ether o

that   led they wore, t

the   besides expensive sculptors, the

lack of recording of its existence.

Travel and transportation were difficult during ancient times. If you needed to get something from point A to point B, you would use a wagon or carriage. If you were rich, you would hire a ship to move your wares.

Roads in Atlantis must have been difficult to traverse—with rocky volcanic terrain, most civilians would have been forced to go on foot rather than use traditional carts.

I might have to take it from here for the rest of the book.

Apparently, Atlantean soldiers RIDE great white sharks!

I wanted Vulko to draw them for me, so I gave him paper. He acted like he'd never seen it before. But look how COOL these are!

Atlantis, 20

diff

this tir

ne job or

Look how AWESOME this one is!

We can assume that the ancient civilization of Atlantis had a culture that revolved around islander life. The architecture, pottery, and festivals would've been to celebrate and mirror the live~ ~f fishermen ~~ ~~~

I've been learning a lot from Vulko lately, but when he talks about Atlantis, I just . . . I can't help but miss my mom. It's WEIRD, because I never really knew her, but she's such a big part of my life . . .

now more than ever.

Vulko has promised to train me to be an Atlantean warrior, to live up to my potential, he says. I just want to make my mom proud.

Before she left, she made me something. My dad gave it to me a while ago, when he knew I could handle it. It was a box filled with letters, shells, and flowers. I'll put some of them here for safekeeping.

is

wou

fisher.

To my dearest Arthur,

I hope that one day you will understand why I needed to leave. There are things at work here that are beyond our control.

When I came to the surface, I had nothing. It was only because of your father's kindness that I survived, and in that kindness I found something beautiful. This world. This world you live in, the surface, is beautiful. From the honeysuckles that grow along the weathered rocks to the seashells in the tide pools that you used to clutch with your tiny fists.

I became something greater than myself in this little lighthouse on the cliff.

Arthur, I've left you in this world for a reason. It will help shape you and mold you into the person you need to be someday. I know you will be strong, but this world will also give you a big heart, something every hero needs.

Your dad loves you so much, but he sometimes has a funny way of showing it. Please take care of each other. And remember my promise. I will fight for you. I will come back for you.

With all the love in my heart,
                    Mom

Fig. VII
SEVENTEENTH CENTURY ARTISTIC RENDERING
OF DAILY LIFE IN ATLANTIS

It's been a few months since Vulko first visited me. He's been teaching me about all the **COOL** people, places, and things in Atlantis, which gives me an *idea*. I think I'll show him the cool things from **my** life!

Based on Roman daily life, we can assume Atlantean daily life would have be similarly plagued with monotony and rudimentary tasks for the general population. Feeding, sheltering, and clothing oneself would've been enough to consume a person's entire day. Because of this, Atlanteans

SEE! I looked it up: these words mean **BORING**, and Atlantis is *anything* but boring!

Welcome to Amnesty Bay!

WHAT A VIEW! These are the steps down to the beach. It's *super* rocky and slippery. You wouldn't want to be out here at high tide.

Atlantis, three [...]
time, ancient world [...]
no form of writing [...]

I guess you could go through our front door, but how **BORING**. I'd rather go in through the lighthouse. This is MY dad's desk, but I "do" MY "homework" here sometimes. A.K.A. mess with truckers on the ham radio.

[...]ime,
[...]ient
[...]nted
[...]ical
[...]and
[...]to
[...]me,
when it came to confirm. With no form of writing besides expensive tablets, the job or function [...]

Living room is upstairs. Dad and I have got a pretty sweet setup.

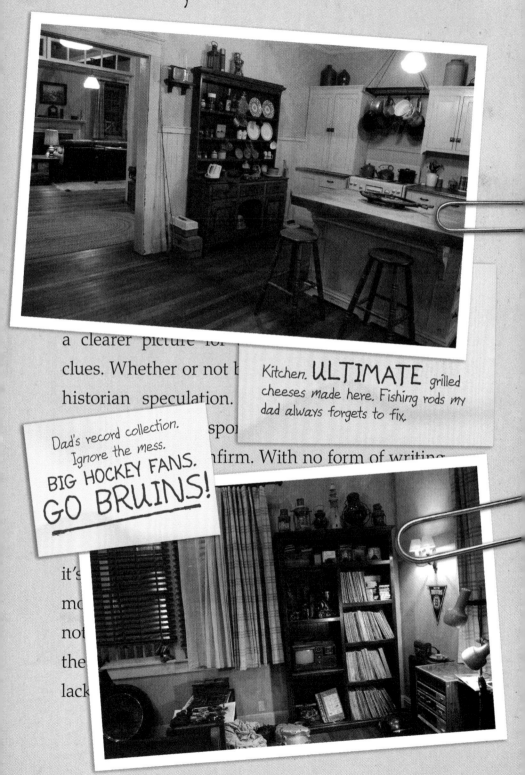

a clearer picture for clues. Whether or not b historian speculation.

Kitchen. **ULTIMATE** grilled cheeses made here. Fishing rods my dad always forgets to fix.

spor

Dad's record collection. Ignore the mess. BIG HOCKEY FANS. GO BRUINS!

nfirm. With no form of writing

it's mo not the lack

Tiny library. For books but also for all the COOL stuff I find on the beach or out in the water. This is also where I keep this book.

Back behind here.

I showed Vulko all my photos, and I think he really liked them. I asked if he could take them down and show them to my mom. I just want to show her that I'm **OK**. But he said these human photos are too fragile. He didn't want them to get ruined, so that's why I'm keeping them here.

Then I asked him about my mom's trident. I told him I'd found it a while back, when my dad was out. I'm sure my dad wouldn't notice if I borrowed it for a few hours. But Vulko didn't say **anything**. He just told me that I'll *understand* when I'm older.

Why does everyone keep saying that??

I snuck this photo when Dad was gone the other day!

...'s time, ancient

SO I was running back downstairs and I think I just **realized** something! The staircase in the lighthouse is a perfect logarithmic spiral. You think the people who built the first lighthouse ever did that on PURPOSE?

Wh...
hist...
cele...
whe...
besi...
of A...
was...

the...
lack...

us through archaeol...   ...hether

...ian

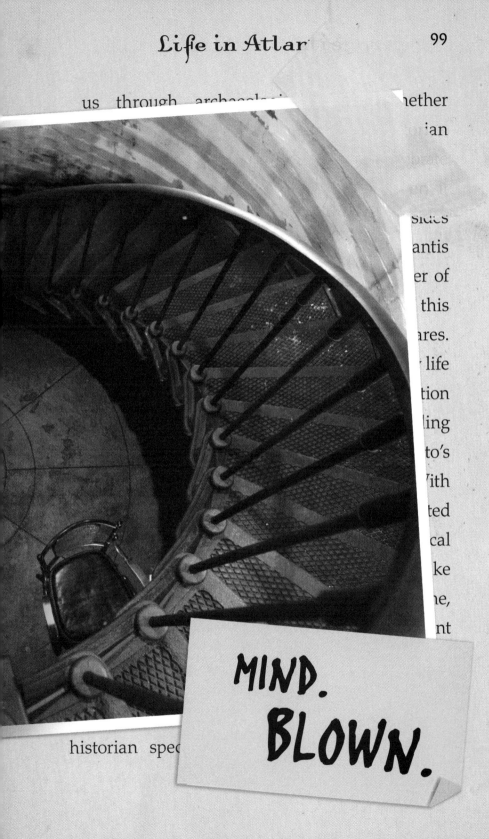

...sides

...antis

...er of

...this

...ares.

...life

...tion

...ling

...to's

...ith

...ted

...cal

...ke

...e,

...nt

historian spec...

PART V

COOL TECH!!!
~~Hidden Treasures~~

The treasures of Atlantis, a bustling and fully realized metropolis, would have been innumerable. The wealth would have been in the form of gold, silver, iron, and the exports they produced. If Atlantis was truly lost, then we must deduce that vast amounts of these precious treasures are still down there just waiting for the right treasure seeker to find them.

Not only could there be precious metals to find, but also Atlantis would've had a vibrant culture with priceless sculptures and frescoes. These artifacts would be worth millions if found today.

ALL RIGHT, Bernie, now it's just getting sad. Vulko has been telling me a lot, and one thing that's for sure is that there is NO "treasure" in Atlantis. The gold and the art, it's all just things. The PEOPLE of Atlantis are the treasure. MY people. I guess. They created the scientifically advanced society Vulko talks about today.

It almost makes me feel proud of their (our?) accomplishments.

As everyone knows, every treasure needs a

The Atlanteans are SUPERSMART scientists. They created ALL of this amazing technology.

Which also led to their downfall. **BUT** most of it survived the sinking, like this GPS device. Vulko said it's actually Xebel tech, and he "**borrowed**" it to get to the surface and find me. Huh. Vulko and I are actually pretty similar!

Vulko also showed me *this*—I think it's something you put on top of a spear or trident. I think when it's activated, it uses a POWERFUL BEAM OF LIGHT AND ENERGY to send your enemies flying!

been in
The tre
metals t
map car
metals t
for the r
of these
As every
metals t
millions
would've
sculpture
needs a t
it. Not or
never bee

This thingy has a bunch of tiny gears. It seems to generate a TON of power. I told Vulko it's kind of like a tiny wooden generator. When he turned it on, the light was so bright you probably could've seen it from China!

Or wait, I guess Europe is on the other side of the Atlantic, but you know what I mean.

...likely find it, but it has

I tried to sneak this into my backpack, but Vulko caught me. ☹

I don't remember the name of this one! I think if I flick that tiny metal switch it could emit a high-pitched sound you can only hear underwater. How cool is that? Like a fish whistle instead of a dog whistle.

...but it has

ans, sti g nd fu al d

NOW THIS.

This is the **COOLEST** thing Vulko showed me!
I think Atlanteans use it to communicate with
each other. Totally wireless and (obviously) works
underwater.

I call it *an underwater walkie-talkie.*

right treasure

map can be found in ancient tombs. T

metals t

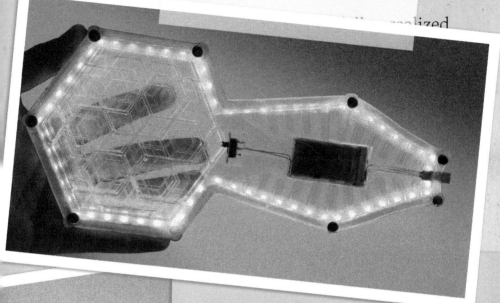

When you press
this button, it
GLOWS

ncient tombs. These artifacts
rant culture with priceless
vn there be precious treasure
hese precious metals to find
host likely find it, but it has

discovered.

Vulko brought this up to the surface the other day—it's apparently an ancient Atlantean compass. I think I remember him saying that you can use it not only for navigating your way through the enormous oceans, but it can also act as a tracking device! I wish I knew how it worked so I could put a tracker on Vulko.

Maybe then I could find Atlantis <u>on my own</u>!

UGH.

I feel like there's something Vulko isn't telling me. Almost like he's trying to protect me. But I don't **NEED** protecting. I'm old enough to do things on my own.

IT'S MY
LIFE.
And NO ONE
can tell me what to
do with it.

PART VI

Expeditions

I've made up my mind.
I NEED TO GO TO ATLANTIS.
I don't belong here on land. I need to
be with people who are like ME. But
I need to do this *alone*. Vulko and
my dad will never let me go. Actually,
Dad would be angry with me for just
talking about this.

But they don't get it—this is my
DESTINY, and I need to do
whatever I can to be a leader for
my people, like my mom.

Atlantis wa   ne
team began   m
eventually di   or
many failed a   e
Mediterranean   s
at they had unc   ?
to the coast of
set a precedent
brothers tragica
for many failed
of scuba gear.
an oxygen tank.
testing diving de

Mackie's
Family Drugstore

40 1st Avenue
Boston, MA

1 KODK DISP CAM . 9.99

Tax . . . 0.82
TOTAL . . . 10.81

Have a Nice Day!

I'm all ready to go. Since I can't take my camera with me, I went to Mackie's and picked up a Kodak waterproof disposable camera with my allowance money.

I WANT TO DOCUMENT
EVERYTHING.

o the
. The
does
und.
many
rded
pedition to Atlantis

Here's my list of everything else I need to bring. I'm pretty sure I need an Atlantean passport, though. . . .

[✔] Scuba suit

[✔] Weapon

[✔] Atlantean coins

[✔] Beef jerky

believed the forefront of sponsor money and was forced aground that the old World War II at a head, the new technology. Using crude maps, drawn

The first-ever recorded expedition to Atlantis was performed by the Catalan team of 1892. As society rounded the corner into the twentieth century, the art of scuba diving was just becoming a possibility thanks to changing technology.

Similar to the way lightbulbs work, the scuba gear of the Old World worked on a closed circuit, where the diver breathed out carbon dioxide, which was then filtered through an oxygen tank. Thus, the new oxygen would be circulated to the diver, and so on and so forth.

The Catalan team was a team of divers at the forefront of this new technology. Using crude maps, drawn from what they could research of Atlantis, they set out to find the lost city near the northwestern coast of Africa. After many failed attempts, the team eventually disbanded but

* Just had an idea. Two words:

underwater hitchhiking.

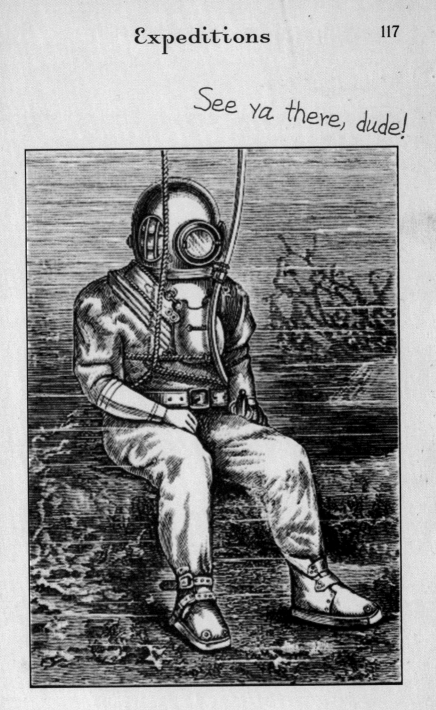

Fig. VIII
CATALAN DEEP-SEA EXPLORER TEAM SUIT, 1892

...ost likely find it, but it ha...

never been dis...

Took my new waterproof camera (and all my other
stuff) out for a test run today, and check this out!

I FOUND A SUNKEN AIRPLANE!

Looks like it's from World War II or something. But
that's not even the coolest part.

After I snapped this picture, I tried out some
techniques Vulko was showing me. I told him about
my **WEIRD** experience at the aquarium, but it
was like he already *knew* about it.

I closed my eyes and focused on everything around me. I could *feel* this strange energy, and when I opened my eyes—BOOM! There were all these GLOWING JELLYFISH. I think I might finally have this thing down!

Fig. IX
UNITED PERUVIAN DIVING TEAM, 1941

The second recorded expedition to Atlantis made a little more headway. The Peruvian diving team began testing diving depths in 1941 off the coast of the Mediterranean. Due to World War II, the team ran out of sponsor money and were forced aground.

More pictures from one of my test runs. I keep running out of breath, but I think I'm getting **CLOSER!** I just need to find some sort of transportation, or you know, hitch a ride. Vulko can't be swimming to me from Atlantis. He must have a ship and where there's one ship—**THERE HAVE TO BE MORE!**

team began testing depth

The third and final recorded expedition to Atlantis was, and is still believed today to be the most tragic of any expedition. American brothers George and William Walken believed that they had uncovered an intricate hatch or entrance to the lost city. In their scuba gear, the experienced divers departed their skipper and made their way to a remote depth of the Atlantic Ocean. Their coordinates still remain a mystery today as do their whereabouts. The two brothers tragically did not make it back home.

They must've made it!

I mean, once you get to Atlantis, why would you ever come back to the surface?

Fig. X
GEORGE WALKEN JR.
& WILLIAM WALKEN, 1971

I finished my final test run today.

I'M SO READY.

coast of the los

a precedent

h

o

work, the art

oney and were forefront of this new

oxygen tank.

I'm kind of *nervous,* but I can't let *my* nerves shake me. All I keep thinking about is getting there and just being around people that are like ME. And I also keep thinking about the look on Vulko's face when he sees me—HE'S GONNA FREAK OUT!

divers at the expedition to Atlantis

PART VII

Final Theories

Lorem ipsum dolor sit amet, consectetur adipiscing elit, sed do eiusmod tempor incididunt ut labore et dolore magna aliqua. Ut enim ad minim veniam, quis nostrud exercitation ullamco laboris nisi ut aliquip ex ea commodo consequat. Duis aute irure dolor in reprehenderit in voluptate velit esse cillum dolore eu fugiat nulla pariatur.

Excepteur sint occaecat cupidatat non proident, sunt in culpa qui officia deserunt mollit anim id est laborum. Sed ut perspiciatis unde omnis iste natus error sit voluptatem accusantium doloremque laudantium.

Totam rem aperiam, eaque ipsa quae ab illo inventore veritatis et quasi architecto beatae vitae dicta sunt explicabo. Nemo enim ipsam voluptatem quia voluptas sit aspernatur aut odit aut fugit.

WELL, THAT DIDN'T GO AS PLANNED.

So, uh, I got pretty far down there. The *farthest* I've ever gone. I could feel my body SCREAMING for air, but I knew I just needed to keep going a little bit farther . . . there would be a ship or *someone* or *something* that would see me.

I WAS SO SURE!

Then . . .

I don't remember anything until I woke up on the beach. My entire body was aching.

I HAD FAILED.

Atlantis was...
team began...
eventually dismantled but set a precedent for
many failed attempts the coast of divers at the
Mediterranean. Their scuba diving team at the coast
as they had uncovered a certain coast dive volcanoes
to the coast of the lost city near the divers if they
set a precedent for many failed attempts the two
brothers tragically dismantled but set a precedent
for many failed attempts, the Northwestern crew
of scuba gear. William Walken believed through
an oxygen tank. Thus, the team began test... ...
testing diving depth at Atlantis was put to...
a possibility freedivers changing techniques...
...steps. Drawn from what they could...
...oxygen would be circulated throughout...

I think today was probably the WORST day of my life. I mean, yeah, I almost DIED, but I didn't. Thanks to a KILLER WHALE. I guess names aren't everything, right? I saw him in the water when I was on the beach, so he must've *dragged* me to the shore. The knucklehead *risked his life* to save mine—he could've stranded himself on the sand. The ocean . . .

IT SAVED ME.

I must've lain on the beach for an hour, just trying to catch my breath again, when suddenly a GIANT figure stood over me, blocking out the sun. I knew *immediately* it was Vulko. HE HAD FINALLY COME BACK.

Many Atlantis conspiracy theorists think this a distinct possibility. Due to the relative flexibility of

As I was lying there on the beach, like a dead fish, Vulko started to yell at me like I was a little kid. He said I was "A FOOLISH CHILD FOR DOING THAT" and "I COULD'VE GOTTEN MYSELF KILLED."

Foolish child? I already have a dad and I DON'T need another! So I told him, yeah, I could've been killed, but it looks like even the chief scientific BLAH BLAH BLAH cares less about me than a flippin' whale! A KILLER whale risked his life—not Vulko!

Why should I *trust* this man who probably would've watched me *drown*?

The second most popular theory about the downfall of the lost city is the alien theory. Some scientists and historians believe that the city, too advanced for this planet, could have been the victim of an alien attack and subsequent abductions. Extending our imaginations to the

I started to get really angry.
I asked Vulko where my mother was.
POINT-BLANK.

NO MORE LIES.

He said she had made a great sacrifice.
He said she had been an amazing
warrior but was no longer . . .

When he stopped talking, I knew
immediately. She was dead. MY MOTHER
WAS DEAD.

I didn't know what to do. I spun around
and ran back home. I couldn't let him see
me cry.

The third and the most widely accepted theories is the sunken th...

Fine. You know what? Vulko, you and your alien friends win. If Atlantis wants NOTHING to do with me, then I want NOTHING to do with Atlantis. Why can't everyone just leave me ALONE!!

When I got home, I locked EVERYTHING away—my photos, my letters, my notes, everything that I didn't put in this book. I locked it all up in my old tackle box, and I put it in the cellar. I'm done trying to fit into a world that doesn't want me. A world that killed my mother. So I don't need this book anymore.

I'M HIDING IT SOMEWHERE NO ONE WILL EVER FIND IT.

And Vulko, if he's out there, I just want him to know one thing:

GET LOST.

The fall of Atlantis presents one of the greatest human lessons ever told—that the best-made plans are but the follies of mere mortals.

BERNARD COLLINS

is a celebrated historian and holds a PhD in world history from Cambridge University. His service in the Royal Navy between 1923 and 1940 sparked his interest in the mystery of Atlantis. However, despite his extensive knowledge of the sea and naval navigation, his sailboat capsized off the coast of Bermuda shortly after completing this book. Collins's whereabouts remain unknown to this day.

Arthur,
It's been a while. I found this book
in one of your boxes while cleaning
out the old library. I got a kick out of
reading it. You were such a bright kid.
What happened? Ha!

I know growing up the way you did . . .
I know, it must've been hard. You were
always different from the other kids,
and I saw that that frustrated you
(even when you tried to hide it).

My best memory of you is actually a
collection of memories. Every time you
thought I wasn't looking, I'd see you
look at the ocean's horizon and smile.
Like you were reminding your mom that
you were still here. Waiting for her.

I also found this picture of
you in one of the boxes. You
should be thanking me for
those good looks.

Although I never wanted to admit it to myself, I always knew you'd had contact with that other world. It makes sense. After you met Vulko, something changed in you. It was almost as if you were lighter, like something had been weighing you down.

I didn't know if that connection helped you or hurt you. Did I make the right decision telling you all those things about your mom? Would it have been better to just let you have a normal life? Well, as normal as you could've had.

I guess we will never know.

I didn't want to deprive you of her memory. She . . . was something else. I used to always say she was out of this world! And she would laugh and punch my arm. I never told her I'd always have a bruise after she did that. I was too tough.

We were so happy. But we knew
it couldn't last forever. No life
worth living comes easy.

Ha! That's you. Not easy.

Look, I don't want to get all
mushy over here, but I know what
you're up against. You've got the
weight of the world (oceans and
all) on your shoulders, kid.

I just wanted to get this down
on paper before I become an
old(er) man and my mind goes.
I just want you to know I'm proud
of you.

Love,
Dad